Bring two of every
living thing into the ark.
Bring male and female
of them into it. They will be
kept alive with you.

Genesis 6:19
(NIrV)

For Zachary and Chera, our children —
and for Spot and Precious and Frisket and Sandy and Alex and Thumper and
all the other little animals who sometimes make our home feel like an ark.

To my nephews Kyle, Jeffrey, and Jordan — M.L.B.

Tales from the Ark

written by David and Chonda Pierce

illustrated by Matt LeBarre

Zonderkidz

Contents

Introduction
All Aboard

P airs of all creatures that have the breath of life in them came to Noah and entered the ark .... (Genesis 7:15).

Long, long ago the greatest animal adventure ever in the history of the world took place in a giant boat known as an ark. Two of every kind of animal obeyed the voice of God and journeyed from the far reaches of the world to find a bed of straw and a dish of water saved especially for them on the ark, where they could rest safe and sound. And then for forty days and forty nights the rains fell, and for many days afterward the waters rose, so that eventually the whole earth was covered like an ocean. But aboard the ark, built by Noah and his sons, everything was nice and dry and comfy—NOT!

How could it be when you have two of every kind of animal in the whole wide world packed into a room a little bigger than a football field? To be honest, it was dark and dank and damp and loud with a symphony of clucks and squawks and grunts. There were big furry animals that snorted and slobbered on anything near them, and little wriggly animals that slithered and wiggled on anything close to them. There was fur and hair and scales and skin all over the rough, uneven floors. There was pushing and shoving, bickering and rolling and swinging and lumbering and gamboling. And, above all, there were the smells (enough said about that—for now).

Yet, they all survived to eventually leave the ark and spread out (finally!) to have families of their own, with lots and lots of little animals to fill the world. But what really happened during that time on the ark? During the time it rained and was tossed about from wave to wave? During the time it stopped raining and just floated about like a duck on a pond?

That's what you'll find out in this book. Here, for the first time, the animals will tell their stories. Here you'll read about the snoring Camel, the very strong Skunk, an Ostrich who defends her feathered friends, a Ferret who gets lost, a Giraffe who just wants some fresh air, and the Turtle Doves who have a dark, scary secret.

It was a very small world then. (How else could you explain a Yak and a Porcupine having a conversation?) But if the ark was a place where the big and the furry bumped up against the light and the feathery, a place where mistakes were made, deeds misunderstood, and near disasters barely avoided, where loose boards were always creaking and top-pling, where black goo (what the Bible calls "pitch") seemed to be everywhere, where water dripped and birds were always flying about and—well, you get the picture—then it was also a place where lessons were learned, where relation-ships were mended, and (because there just happened to be a storm going on) where God's presence was constant and con-stantly remembered by all.

So hug your pets (you many even want to invite them under the covers to snuggle tonight—maybe not), definitely grab your umbrella, and turn the pages. And if at some point the room begins to rock and tilt and sway, don't worry, just hold on tighter (to your covers, umbrella, pets) because what you are about to read are not more simple stories plotted and written merely to help you fall asleep, but rather they are well-traveled, weathered, rustic, and waterlogged Tales from the Ark!

Chapter 1

Abraham the Polar Bear Takes a Walk … a Run … and a Ride …

All around was thick, fluffy, white, and cold snow. And whenever Abraham the Polar Bear would make a line of footprints in the fresh white snow, more white would simply fall from the sky and fill the holes until the ground was completely smooth. This was the perfect home for a polar bear. Here he had plenty of fish from the nearby river whenever he got hungry, plenty of snow, and plenty of cold. Perfect!

So why was Abraham thinking about leaving? And of all things, going to a place where there was no snow? Because God said, "Go."

Abraham had always listened to God before. Sometimes God would tell him, "There are fish in the bend of the river, just beyond that tree," or "Better make yourself a nice, cozy hole because more snow will fall tonight." God always took care of Abraham, so Abraham always tried to obey God. Now, it seemed, God wanted him to go to a far-off place. Abraham sighed deeply, and the cold air whistled through his nose and filled his big chest. He loved this place, and he knew obeying God wasn't going to be easy.

Abraham was thinking so hard about obeying God that he didn't even notice the rock that he tripped over. He slid and rolled down a giant hill and then laughed as the snow filled his ears and nose. At the bottom, he shook off the snow and thought, "Okay, I'll go. But it's going to be hard to beat this kind of fun." He shook off the extra white from his coat and began to walk to a place where there was no snow.

For a long time Abraham walked, until the white turned to green and the cold was gone. He stopped to rest when suddenly he heard, "Wha-a-a-at are you doing he-e-e-ere?"

Abraham turned his eyes to the top of a high, rocky cliff to see a mountain goat. "I have somewhere to go," Abraham answered.

"Whe-e-e-ere are you go-o-o-ooing?" the goat asked.

"I'm not sure," Abraham replied.

"Then ho-o-ow will you know whe-e-en you get there?" the goat questioned.

Abraham didn't have an answer.

The mountain goat laughed. "Silly bear. You'll sta-a-arve, and the heat will ki-i-ll you.

Go-o-o home,
silly be-a-ar."

Abraham tried
to shake the
words from his head like he would snow
from his coat, and ran away from the mountain goat—not
because he was afraid the goat would hurt him. He ran
because he didn't want to listen to the goat and maybe dis-
obey God. After all, going back to where it was white, fluffy,
and cold sounded pretty good to him right now. But Abraham
ran on until, before long, he was just a small, white spot on a
giant sea of green.

Day after day, Abraham walked past colorful trees and flowers, more bright and speckled than a fish's back. Sometimes he'd stop to watch flying, buzzing things that made him dizzy as they zipped from flower to flower.

But in all this beauty, Abraham was miserable. The sun was too hot on his heavy, white coat, the air was too hot, even the ground he was walking on was too hot. Oh yes, he was miserable, but still he walked on.

One day, as he sat under a giant tree, he remembered that old goat's words: "You don't belong here." And underneath the tree, in the hot shade, he turned those words over and over in his mind like tiny pebbles, until he saw a large "rock" walk by. He leaned forward and studied the rock and soon discovered that it had four feet and a little head.

"What are you?" Abraham asked.

"I'm a turtle," the creature answered. "Are you a polar bear too?"

"Why, er, yes I—too?" Abraham said, more excited than he'd been in days. "You mean you've seen others like me?"

"Just one," the turtle replied. "She was beautiful and very kind. I've seen many strange and wonderful animals recently. What about you? Where are you headed?"

Abraham sighed. "I don't really know, but I've been going that way," and he pointed.

"Great!" said the turtle. "That's where I am going. You can follow me, but you will have to keep up."

So Abraham followed his new friend. The slower pace felt good because the bear was feeling very, very warm.

Before long, Abraham heard voices—lots of them, laughing, talking, and shouting. They were the sounds of animals whinnying, oinking, clucking, barking, tweeting, and hissing. Soon he and the turtle came to an opening in the woods where he saw all kinds of animals alongside a huge, wooden thing—higher than any of the trees around it.

This thing was as big as a mountain and made from cut trees, more than Abraham could have counted. But the strangest things were these creatures walking around on two legs. Some were carrying straw and others were pounding the sides of this huge wooden thing with stones, while others were spreading a thick, black goo along the object's rough wooden belly. A large opening was cut into the side, and the animals were walking up the ramp that led into the dark hole.

Abraham pointed to one of the beings who had a big bucket of black goo in one hand. "What is that?" Abraham asked the turtle.

"Those are humans," answered the turtle. "Sometimes they like to pick you up and pet your nose."

Then Abraham noticed that one of the humans, an older man with a long, white beard, was waving to him and walking his way. He was about to wave back when the human whacked his head against a board, then kicked over a bucket of the black goo, and hopped around on one leg for a bit. Abraham smiled and suddenly had a good feeling about these humans. "This is where I belong," he suddenly thought. "This is where—"

Right then, in the heat of the day, Abraham froze, for suddenly he was face-to-face with another polar bear. And she was beautiful.

"My name is Sarah," the new bear said. "What's yours?"

"I . . . ah . . er ah—"

"His name is Abraham," the turtle offered. "You'd think he'd never seen a polar bear before."

Abraham cleared his throat as he waved an arm in the direction of the ramp and said to Sarah, "Shall we?"

Sarah giggled and walked with Abraham toward the ramp.

Looking up and studying this huge, wooden thing up close now, Abraham asked, "What is this thing, anyway?"

"I heard the man with the white beard call it an ark," said a little black-and-white animal that didn't smell good to Abraham.

"An ark?" Abraham said. "So what does an ark do?"

Just then a pair of gray turtle doves landed on the back of a hippo that was trying to push its way through the crowd. The doves flapped their wings and turned in little circles. One of the doves cleared its throat and said, "An ark floats."

Abraham just shrugged and smiled at Sarah as they moved at a turtle's pace closer to the opening. Just before he entered, he took one last look up the side of the huge ark and believed the thing must surely reach all the way to the clouds. That's when a single drop of rain hit him in the eye. He thought about what the dove had said. "It floats?" he repeated. "And just what's so great about that?"

But before anyone could answer, the hippopotamus said, "Please hurry! Please hurry! This is an emergency!" And the line pushed forward. Even the turtle moved faster to see what could be so important. . . .

Chapter 2
A Little Help, Please ... the ARK IS SINKING!

There was no doubt about it as far as Jehoshaphat the Yak was concerned: the ark was sinking!

Jehoshaphat was eating a little straw and minding his own business when he heard a strange noise: *Blub, blub, blub*. He looked into the empty stall next to his and saw water bubbling through a crack between the boards.

While the water bubbled in and formed a shiny puddle around his hooves, Jehoshaphat talked to God.

"Dear God, this is Jehoshaphat. I have been on the ark getting ready for the trip. But now I have a problem. You see, there's a hole in the bottom of the ark. If you would, please send help. I think we need an 'ark repair kit.' Thank you, God."

Jehoshaphat already felt better. He took another bite of straw, and as the water got deeper, a plan formed in his brain. But for the plan to work, he would first need to find Noah.

Blub, blub, blub. Jehoshaphat would have to move fast.

Jehoshaphat walked as quickly as he could, his long, flowing hair sweeping the floor as he moved. He moved along the bottom level of the ark, past the elephants, camels, horses, polar bears (he nodded to the white creatures, because he had never seen a polar bear before), and his cousins the buffalo, until finally he was at the ramp that led up to the second level.

The wooden ramp creaked beneath his weight, and his hooves clip-clopped loudly. He would have made it to the top if it hadn't been for the hippopotamus.

"Sorry to take up so much room," said the hippo. His voice was as tiny and squeaky as his body was round and wide. "As soon as I can find my stall, I'll be out of everyone's way. I've searched this ark from top to bottom, and I can't find my name anywhere. And this is somewhat of an emergency, so if you could please help me … Noah said—"

"Noah?" Jehoshaphat interrupted. "Have you seen Noah?"

The hippo nodded. "Only a few moments ago. He was on the upper level."

"I would like to help you, Mr. Hippo," Jehoshaphat said, "but I have my own emergency to deal with right now." As he started to walk away, Jehoshaphat noticed a giant tear spill from the hippo's eye and roll down his big nose.

"Please don't cry," the yak begged. And Jehoshaphat didn't know how to stop a hippo from leaking any more than he knew how to stop an ark from leaking. "Listen," he said, with all the excitement that comes with a new idea, "it's important that I find Noah. How about if we search for him and your stall at the same time?"

"Oh, thank you!" the hippo whimpered through his tears. A wide grin—one that showed all the gaps between his teeth—spread across his face. Then the hippo turned his head just a little and listened. "By the way, what's that *blub, blub, blub* sound coming from below?"

The yak's eyes bugged out. "We'd better run!" he said to the hippo. But the hippo had already turned and bolted past the goats, gazelles, foxes, and llamas to another ramp that led even higher, up to the third level. He made such a wide turn that he almost tipped over and nearly squashed a pair of laughing hyenas (who thought the whole thing was hilarious). Fortunately for the hyenas, the hippo caught his balance and then thundered on up the ramp, leaving Jehoshaphat way behind.

Jehoshaphat finally caught up to the hippo on a narrow path between the stalls when they were stopped by a stinging little voice: "Hey! Watch it!"

The yak and the hippo turned at the same instant and, with their hind ends, knocked over two little gray prickly porcupines. The porcupines rolled down the center aisle like two pincushions—at least until a wooden post stopped them.

Mr. Porcupine got up, rubbed the back of his head, and said, "We would have preferred a

handshake. So what are you big guys
doing up here, anyway?"

"We're looking for the hippo's
home," the yak said, "and for
Noah and—"

"Well, his home isn't up here,"
Mrs. Porcupine interrupted.

"Why not?" responded the
hippo.

"Because, silly," replied Mrs. Porcupine, smiling and blinking her long lashes, "all you big animals are on the lower level—with the polar bears."

"The lower level!?" the hippo and Jehoshaphat said at the same instant.

"Ssssaayy!" sang Mr. Porcupine. "Do you think you could take my wife and me down to see the polar bears? Noah said if ever we get the chance, we should—"

"Noah?" Jehoshaphat interrupted. "Have you seen Noah?"

"Yes. He was heading to the lower level," Mr. Porcupine squeaked. "You must have just missed him."

"Now we're getting somewhere!" the hippo shouted. "Let's go!"

The hippo bounded across the ark's deck, scattering small animals to each side and creating a wide path behind him for Jehoshaphat to follow.

"Hey, what about us?" said Mr. Porcupine.

"We'll come back and give you a tour later," said Jehoshaphat. And he ran after the hippopotamus.

When Jehoshaphat finally made it to the lower level, he was greeted by the smell of some very damp straw: Things were getting wetter. He found the hippo chatting excitedly with the polar bears; he seemed to have forgotten all about finding his home. Jehoshaphat looked from one end of the ark to the other, but he saw no sign of Noah.

Sadly, he walked over to the stall where the leak was and began to eat some of the dry straw that was up higher. *Blub, blub, blub* went the water. "Why," he wondered, "would God allow Noah and his family to work so long and so hard to build an ark, and then let it sink on the first day?"

Then, as startling as a clap of thunder, the hippo bellowed, "That's it! Thank you, Jehoshaphat! You're a great friend."

Jehoshaphat nearly choked on his straw. "W-W-What did I do?" Jehoshaphat asked.

"My home! You found my home!"

The hippo looked up, and Jehoshaphat followed his gaze. On a board, just about eye-level for the hippo, and at one time covered by the straw that the yak had just eaten, was carved the word *Hippopotamus*. The happy hippo turned completely around and backed into the empty stall. He kept backing up until his tail bumped against the wall. Then suddenly, without any sort of announcement, his four squatty legs slipped out from under him and, with a thud, he plopped to the floor. The whole ark shook, and the hippo totally covered the tiny hole where the water blubbed up.

"Oh boy!" the hippo shouted. "This is so cool and wet! Perfect! I think I'll just sit right here for a while." He rested his

head on the cool boards. "The last time I was this tired," he added, "I didn't move for forty days and forty nights."

The ark was saved! Jehoshaphat was so happy that he jumped for joy.

"Thank you for finding my home, Jehoshaphat," the hippo said, his voice already sounding sleepy.

"And thank you, God, for sending a big 'ark repair kit,'" Jehoshaphat whispered.

As the hippo slept, it seemed nothing could stir him from his spot, not even the not-so-little problem with Midian the Camel. . . .

Chapter 3

Good Night, Gideon ... Or Maybe Not

Gideon the Beaver crawled deeper into the thick straw, but it would take more than straw to block out the *rattle-rattle-caargh!* sound coming from the stall next to him. When the sleeping camel next door breathed in, the noise wasn't too bad, just a swooshing sound like wind blowing through the holes in a stack of sticks. But when he blew air out, past teeth and gums and lips, then there were knocks

and rattles, whistles and clicks the likes that Gideon had never heard before.

Gideon pulled his head from the straw (since it wasn't doing much good anyway) and stared at Midian the Camel, who lay in a humped heap on the straw floor next to him. The camel inhaled—swoosh!—and then exhaled—rattle-rattle-caargh! Once the rattle was so loud that a pitchfork Noah had left leaning against some hay bales fell over. And another time a stack of loose boards tipped over and crashed to

the floor with a bang like a hammer. Except for the hippopotamus, no one was going to get any sleep tonight. The beaver
covered both ears with his paws and disappeared deeper into
the straw.

"Gideon," a voice called out, "you have to do something!"

Gideon pulled his head from its hiding place and saw a
glowing bright spot in the air—a fire-
fly—twinkling overhead. "Why
me?" he asked.

"Because God has given you a
special gift—the perfect gift to solve
this problem," said the firefly. "But
please hurry, because none of us can get
any sleep around here!" And then the
firefly zipped away in a flash.

"What gift?" Gideon called out
after her,

but the firefly was already gone. "All I can do is chew wood," he said to the sleeping camel, as if the camel were paying attention. "How can that stop—"

Swoosh! Rattle, rattle, caargh! went the camel.

Gideon kept thinking and clicking his teeth, and before long, he had a plan.

For Gideon's plan to work, it was important for Mr. and Mrs. Sheep to help out. "Now, you just stand right there," Gideon told the two sheep, "and don't move."

"How long do we have to stand here?" Mrs. Sheep asked.

Gideon thought about the question and then said, "Until Midian wakes up."

"This doesn't sound like such a great idea to me," Mr. Sheep added.

But Gideon was already snuggling up on his straw bed, and in just a few moments, with the two sheep and their thick wool blocking all the noise that came from the mouth of the camel, the tired beaver fell sound asleep.

But he didn't get to sleep for very long. Because soon he was startled from his nap by Mrs. Sheep's announcement: "This is just not working!"

"What's the matter?" said Mr. Sheep.

"What's the matter?!" exclaimed Mrs. Sheep. "I'll tell you what's the matter. The matter is all over my coat! Sorry, Gideon, but you'll have to find someone else to help you." And with that, Mrs. Sheep marched off, leaving a long squiggly trail of camel sneeze on the floor of the ark as she walked away.

In the meantime, Midian the Camel kept on sleeping: *Swoosh! Rattle, rattle, caargh!*

So, tired and surrounded by funny noises, Gideon thought once again about what the firefly had said about the special gift that God had given him. And with a click of his teeth, he thought of another plan—only this one seemed much simpler.

With all his strength and energy (and just a touch of bravery), he set about in a whirlwind upon some old boards he'd found. His sharp front teeth clicked and clacked as he became a blur of fur. Scampering all around the sleeping camel, his razor-sharp teeth cut and hewed the boards so that wood chips flew out in all directions.

When Gideon was finished, he called out to the camel, "Hey, Midian, wake up and try this on for size!" The beaver pointed to a lovely little square box with an egg-shaped hole in one side.

"What is it?" the camel asked.

"That," said Gideon, as he proudly swiped the edges of his two front teeth with one paw, "is a 'snore box.'"

"A snore box? Never heard of it," said Midian.

"That's because I just made it up."

"How does it work?"

"Just lie down facing this way," the beaver instructed. "And stick your head inside the hole."

The camel did just that. "Okay," came the muffled voice of Midian, and Gideon could just barely hear him. "Now what?"

"Now . . . go to sleep."

In no time at all, Midian fell fast asleep, and Gideon had to really listen to hear the slightest click or snort or rattle. The snore box worked! And when Gideon made the announcement, all the animals rejoiced with every sort of *bray, whinny, bark,* and *baa.* And the firefly lit up the whole room in a happy, green glow. Gideon was happy too. But all he wanted to do was rest. So he pushed and fluffed and piled up his straw bed until it was the softest it had ever been. And with a big sigh, the hero—the one who had used the special gift that God had given to him—sank deep into the straw and took a long nap.

And he would have slept much longer if it wasn't for the ferret who ran back and forth across the floor and over Gideon's tail a few times, obviously upset about something. . . .

Chapter 4
Moses the Ferret Searches High and Low

It was a dark and stormy night on the ark (again!) when the problems all started for Moses the Ferret. The ark rocked so much one way and then the other that Zipporah, Moses' wife, slid right off her straw bed, down the ramp to the next level, and just disappeared into the sea of other animals. Gone!

"Zipporah?" Moses called out, looking across the empty spot on the hay next to him. He climbed to the top of a hay bale and sat upright on his hind legs and called out again, first to his left and then to his right. But there was no answer. With panic in his voice, Moses turned to his friends and cousins—the mink, the weasel, and Joshua the Hamster—and said, "We have to find her! Can you help me?"

"We'll help," Joshua trumpeted. "Won't we, friends? Let's go."

"Help what?" asked a spotted rat with a long pink tail.

"We'll help Moses find his wife, Zipporah!" So together, in a large group, they set out, wandering about the ark. They searched high—where the birds and the giraffes hung out. And they searched low—where the crocodiles splashed around in the very bottom where the hippos napped. But Zipporah was nowhere to be found.

Every chance he got, Moses would stop and ask someone if they'd seen his wife. "Excuse me, Mr. Porcupine. You haven't happened to have seen my wife wandering about, have you?"

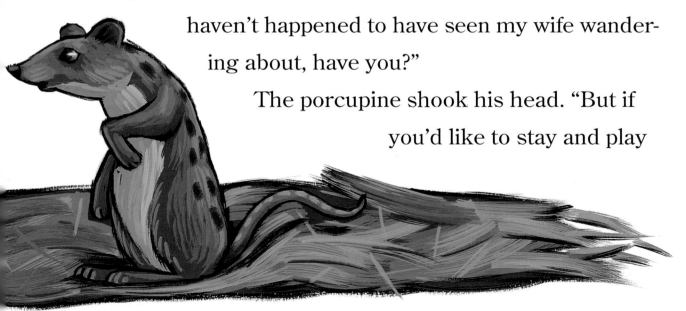

The porcupine shook his head. "But if you'd like to stay and play we can take turns," he said. The two porcupines were seesawing on a long plank balanced on a hay bale, up and down, up and down, the wind blowing through their . . . prickly pins.

But Moses moved on and then asked a big rhinoceros, who had barrel hoops hanging from the horn at the end of his nose. A red fox was playing loop-the-rhino-horn. "No," answered the rhinoceros. "But why don't you stay and play for a while? You can look later." Moses thought the game looked really fun, but he had to shake his head no.

Onward Moses and his band went, asking everyone he saw if they had seen Zipporah, but the answer was always the same: No. Then he stopped and asked a cow, who, in the golden light of the oil lamps, looked almost golden herself. "How now brown cow?" said Moses.

The small brown cow turned and blinked her long, beautiful lashes. When she saw the ferret, she giggled and said, "My, you sure are a cute little creature."

"Thank you very much," said Moses, "but I was looking for my wife, Zipporah. You haven't seen her wandering about, have you?"

The cow just kept smiling (and giggling). "No, but you're

welcome to stay here and see if she comes by." Then the cow pointed with her nose to a big pile of straw in the corner of her stall. "There's plenty of room for you and your friends." She giggled again. "We could play and have all sorts of fun."

Just then the spotted rat with the long pink tail tugged at the ferret's fur. "This doesn't sound too bad, Mo. Dry straw, warm straw, and," now the rat leaned in closer to Moses so he couldn't be overheard, and pointed discreetly to the cow, "I heard these things have an endless supply of sweet, warm milk." The rat licked his lips and rubbed his tummy. "So what do you say? Why don't we just park it here for a while?" The rat twitched its whiskers in a friendly sort of way.

Moses frowned. He had to find Zipporah. And besides, to him the place was too big, too noisy (close by a camel snored loudly), too dark, and too dangerous. He figured one cow could squash a ferret pretty easily if she happened to forget he was napping in the straw. And just as he was thinking about how clumsy cows could be, this golden calf turned about and knocked over a small table, that knocked over a barrel, that rolled across the floor and hit a pole, that shook a bale of hay from the loft. The hay fell onto one end of the see-saw where the porcupines were playing—sending one of the porcupines into the air and on top of the rhino, who yelped and bolted and, with horn down, charged and parted the sea of animals that filled the floor, and out the door he kept going. And there—at the end of the long clearing left by the rhino— Moses could see Zipporah.

"There she is, Moses!" yelled Joshua.

And Moses, seeing Zipporah, chirped and chittered the way ferrets do when they get too excited. He was so glad he had passed by the porcupines, the rhino, and the cow (even though it looked like they were having lots of fun) or he may have never found what God had intended for him: Zipporah, his wife, his *promised hand.*

Although the trip started out a bit bumpy for Moses and Zipporah, eventually everything seemed to fall into place. At least they didn't have to deal with a big, mean gorilla. . . .

Chapter 5

Is There Enough Room on This Ark for a Goose and a Gorilla?

Deborah the Zebra had wonderful black-and-white stripes, just like a zebra is supposed to. And she had an unusually long, flowing tail that swept the bottom of the ark whenever she walked. But what Deborah did better than anyone else on the ark was answer questions. To the zebra, everything was black-and-white, so everyone lined up to ask her things.

"How did the leopard get its spots?" asked a panther, who was sleek and pretty, but all brown and without a single spot.

"How much wood *can* a woodchuck chuck?" asked a little furry woodchuck, who stood up on his hind legs to get Deborah's attention.

"Why *did* the chicken cross the road?" clucked a hen without a grin.

After each question, Deborah would first twist her face into a frown and study the ceiling, as if she were thinking really hard, but really she was listening to God. It wasn't that she was trying so hard to hear Him—that was the easy part. The hard part was not to hear all the *grunts* and *oinks* and *snorts* and *chorts* of those who crowded in around her. When she was ready to answer, her face would relax into a very pleasant one, so pleasant that oftentimes, when Noah was around, he'd have to reach out and scratch her between the ears.

But the toughest question of all that day came from Jael the Goose. With a *cluck* and a *honk* she asked Deborah, "How do you move a 350-pound ape?"

Deborah frowned and asked, "Is Sisera the Gorilla being a pest again?"

The goose nodded and said, "He lies in the middle of the floor, right where I like to waddle."

"Hmmm," Deborah said, thinking for a moment. "Does he do this a lot?"

"I haven't waddled in days," confessed the goose.

Deborah thought some more. She twisted her face up into a horrible expression and kept it that way until she had an answer. It was her smile that let everyone know this. "There is a way," she said to the goose, "but you'll have to be very, very brave to do it."

Jael pulled her feathered wings back, stuck out her chest, and said, "I'm a goose, not a chicken." The chicken next to her clucked at the insult. "Nothing personal, chicken," said Jael.

Then Deborah leaned in close to tell Jael the plan that God had given her, a plan that would move even a lazy ape.

The next day, when Jael went for a morning waddle, there was Sisera, the big gorilla, all stretched out on the floor so that no one could pass.

Jael considered the plan Deborah had given her, but she thought she'd try talking to the gorilla one more time. "Excuse me, Mr. Sisera, Mr. Gorilla," said Jael. "Can I pass by you? Just need to get by. Just let me slip right through here, and I'll be on my way, my friendly gorilla."

But the gorilla didn't even say hello to Jael. He just lay there, yawning and stretching, picking off fleas and putting them in his mouth. "It's rude to eat in front of someone that way," Jael boldly said.

And for just a brief moment, Jael believed that maybe the gorilla was going to be kind after all, that she wouldn't have to go through with her plan, because he stood up, and if she could have waddled fast enough, she could have slipped past him. But in a moment, and with a great big yawn, the gorilla plopped down again. He was just turning over, getting comfortable.

For a long time Jael watched Sisera eat
and sleep, eat and sleep, eat and sleep. That
did it. She was through talking. Now she was
waiting for the perfect
moment to put Deborah's
plan into action—and to build
up her courage. Finally, the time
came when the gorilla stood up
again. First, he stretched up,
reaching high, and then he
stretched down, bending over.
And when he bent over, Jael
took off and, just as she had
planned it in her mind,
sunk her

pointed bill right into the biggest, softest target the gorilla offered.

With a giant gorilla yelp, Sisera shot through the ark—quite unlike the lazy gorilla Jael had always known. And Jael, quite pleased with the way her plan had gone, waddled back to her home, packed a big lunch, and headed out for an even longer waddle. The first place she was going to go was back to see Deborah. She couldn't wait to tell her all about how the plan had worked, and about how fast a big, lazy gorilla could move.

Lazy gorillas aren't much good for anything but taking up space, and God can help with those sorts

of problems, if you're patient. Giant birds that can't fly—like an ostrich—are an entirely different story. . . .

Chapter 6
Looks Like the Goo's on You, Hyena

Since Haman the Hyena first set paw on the ark, he had endured one simple problem—a problem that seemed to grow with each passing day, a problem that flittered through his mind as ever present and ever elusive as the birds—because the problem was the birds. The finches, the blue jays, the turtle doves—they were all driving him batty. And even though there were plenty of things for a laughing hyena to laugh about on the ark, such as the day the hippo almost tipped over and squashed him or the time the giraffe knocked his noggin on a rafter, just the way these birds seemed to be redecorating the whole ark with all this–

Plop!

The hyena felt something from above land on the end of his nose—again! Sure enough, there, at the end of his nose, was the latest sign of another flying creature. He cleaned himself up with some straw as always, and as he did so, he made a plan to end this mess the birds were making.

Meanwhile, on the bottom deck of the ark—not far from the polar bears—and while everyone else slept, Esther the Ostrich was trying to fly. She stood in a large open area, raised one leg, and flapped her heavy wings. And even though she never lifted up off the floor even the tiniest bit, there, below in the dark ark, she almost believed she could do it.

Haman's plan was brilliant (at least *he* thought so). First, he would gather all the birds together into their flocks and coveys and gaggles. Then he would invite them all to a get-together at the polar bears' place. (Everyone loved going to the polar bears' place, and Haman was certain they wouldn't mind a little company.) And while they were gone, he would take some of the black goo that Noah and his sons were always using—

that stuff that seemed to stick to everything—and rub down the floor. Then he'd take some bread crumbs and sprinkle them all around. And when the birds flew to the bread crumbs, their tiny feet would stick to the floor, and they wouldn't be able to fly. And if they couldn't fly, they wouldn't be able to ... well, "decorate" the ark. He laughed at his plan—but then again he laughed at most everything. (He was a laughing hyena after all.)

And his plan might have worked, too, except that he shared it with someone who didn't think it was all that clever.

"Now let me get this straight," said Esther the Ostrich, who was on her way to the polar bears' place when the hyena stopped her. "So *every* bird on the ark will be stuck in the goo?"

"That's right," laughed Haman. "Our little feathered friends will be grounded! Flightless! No more flying, no more bombing!" He laughed some more. "Good plan, huh?"

The ostrich thought about this and nodded and said, "As a matter of fact, it's a brilliant plan. Thanks for sharing it with me."

The hyena shrugged and said, "Don't mention it. I figured us big guys are getting tired of those little things flapping around and—you know—dotting the eyes and crossing the T's."

"I understand," said Esther.

"And another reason I told you about this plan, is that I could use a little help."

"Help? From me? How could I possibly help?"

Haman nodded and stepped closer to Esther and said, "You see, I found some of that black goo stuff in some jars."

"Yes."

"Only the jars are up on this shelf too high for me to reach. Well, I saw you walking this way and said to myself, 'Now there is someone who can reach a top shelf if she had to.' Am I right?"

"I do have a pretty good view from up here," Esther said proudly, holding her head high.

"Then if you don't mind, perhaps you could pass one of those jars down to me and I'll get started—with the plan." Haman tipped his head in the direction of some jars on a high shelf.

"You mean one of these jars?" Esther asked, nudging one of the pots with her beak.

"Yeah. Oh, be careful. Those things are heavy and if they fall—" Just then Haman noticed something about the big animal he was talking to that he hadn't noticed before: "Hey," he said, with a bit of surprise in his voice, and pointing to Esther's wings, "are those feathers?" The ostrich flapped and stood up on her tiptoes, coming as close to flying as she ever would, and with her beak, she nudged one of the jars too far, just like the hyena had warned about. The jar toppled over the edge and crashed to the floor, splattering black goo up

and all over the bewildered hyena. He rubbed two holes for his eyes and looked up at the giant bird through his new, sleek black coat. "You're one of them, aren't you?" he said.

Esther flapped her wings and said, "Most definitely. Now, if you'll excuse me, I have some family to visit. The polar bears live this way, right?" And Esther sort of flapped as she walked, almost as if she were flying. "I can't wait to see Cousin Blue Jay, Cousin Owl, Cousin Turtle Dove, Cousin . . ." And Esther disappeared, naming all the members of her family who would often fly down to visit with her on rainy nights.

Haman plopped down into a black gooey puddle, disappointed that his plan had failed. Still, he couldn't help himself. Pretty soon he started laughing. Not that anything was especially funny, but only because he was a laughing hyena, after all.

For a long time the hyena laid there, feeling stickier and stickier and thinking things couldn't get much worse. That is, until one day when a very strong skunk showed up. . . .

Chapter 7
Samson the Super Strong Skunk

Sometimes Samson the Skunk was too strong for his own good.

He was very proud of his sleek black coat, but he was most proud of the wide, white streak down the middle, as white as the fur of the polar bears. (He was always quick to point this part out to everyone he met.)

It was the sight of this white stripe that often put fear into the hearts of those closest to him and what caused most of the trouble on this particular day.

On lazy, rainy days Samson liked to have fun by chasing the elephants from one side of the ark to the other—just because he could. He'd sneak up on one of the giant animals and tickle its leg with his tail. At first the elephant would giggle (or snort) until it would look down and see little Samson. Then with a big trumpet blast, the elephant would bolt from its stall and move as far away as it possibly could. Samson would just laugh and then waddle on over to visit the Yak, and the same thing would happen all over again. This little skunk could move them all (except for the Hippos, and only because they slept the whole time). No animal was too big for Samson to move. Yes, Samson was a very strong one, and everyone on the ark knew it. And most of all, Samson was very glad that everyone knew it.

Then one day Samson met a Fox named Delilah. Now Delilah was well

aware of Samson's strength—and she didn't like it at all.
Mainly because she'd nearly gotten trampled one day. She
had been down visiting the polar bears, and the little skunk had the elephants and rhinos and
yaks racing from one side of the ark to the
other. So on this particular
day she cornered

Samson and said, "For such a little guy, you sure make things happen around here. What's your secret?"

But Samson only laughed and said, "No time to talk now. Got a buffalo to budge. See you!" And he was gone, just like that. Delilah didn't have to listen too hard to hear the sounds of a stampede coming from below.

The next day, Delilah met Samson while he was resting. "Tell me, Samson," she began. "All those big animals, from here to there, loud, noisy, nasty. How do you do it?"

Samson, feeling in a talkative mood that day just grinned, curled his black-and-white tail about his nose and said, "It's in the stripe."

"The stripe?"

"Yeah. You seen anybody else with a stripe like this?"

Delilah thought for a moment. "The zebra."

"Too many stripes," Samson stated matter-of-factly. "Just one big stripe like this makes a statement."

"What statement?" asked the fox.

"YOU BETTER MOVE!" the skunk said with a laugh. "Now if you don't mind, I'm going to take a nap, and then I have some bears to relocate." So the skunk curled himself up in a corner, wrapped his long black-and-white tail about his head and began to snooze.

That's when Delilah called out her friends, the ground hog, the raccoons, the aardvarks, the dingoes, and everyone else who'd lived with the fear of being squished when Samson riled up the bigger animals. Quietly, they surrounded Samson as he slept, and the raccoon was the first to whisper, "So what do we do?"

Delilah, who was as sly as Samson was strong, looked about the area and, as quick as a fox, ran from here to there and back again, bringing a bucket clutched between her teeth. *I shay vee ghet whid uf sha shipe.*

"What?" whispered everyone.

Delilah set down the bucket of black goo that Noah and his sons were all the time dabbing here and there and said more clearly, "I say we get rid of the stripe."

So carefully with paws and claws full of the black goo, the animals began to cover the sleeping skunk until the stripe disappeared and Samson might have passed for nothing more than a mink or an otter or a ferret—anything but a skunk. And the goo was so icky and sticky that it'd take a . . . well, it'd take a flood to wash it all off.

When Samson awoke, he made his routine trip to the bottom level and waddled from one big animal to the next, but nothing happened. The moose wouldn't move, the walruses wouldn't waddle, the camels wouldn't even cringe. He couldn't even get a squeak from the mice. Whatever strength Samson had had before was now gone. He was puzzled until he happened to glance over his shoulder. His stripe had disappeared!

Blinded by his own sadness, Samson figured he had some explaining to do—especially to God. He leaned against the giant leg of one of the elephants and said in a weak voice, "God, I know I've been a bit selfish and prideful about my strength, my stripe, the whole smelly skunk thing—okay, a lot selfish and prideful. I wasn't thinking right and—"

"Hey," called the elephant, "who's down there?"

"It's just me."

"Me who?"

"Samson the Skunk."

With those words, the mighty elephant began to tremble. Samson felt the animal's massive legs quake as if they could no longer hold the giant body. What he didn't know was that the elephants had a plan of their own if he should ever show up again. With a careful and steady aim, Mrs. Elephant blasted Samson with enough water to bathe him for a year (especially since he didn't take that many baths

in a year anyway). The force of the spray tumbled Samson into the open, where it was Mr. Elephant's turn to do the same. Each of the giant animals took turns hosing Samson from one side of the ark to the other, so that the water crashed down upon the little skunk's head and back for a long, long time.

When the elephants were all watered out, Samson rolled to his feet, shook himself dry, took one look at his tail and waddled away—happy. *Funny thing about that goo,* he thought. *It may be sticky, but with enough water, it will wash right off. I guess that's why Noah keeps so much extra on hand.*

So with a line of wet footprints trailing behind, Samson returned home, washed clean and carrying his big, beautiful, strong stripe on his back. "Thank you, God," Samson said, in a big, strong voice.

Samson realized, before it was too late, that God had given him the gift of strength—to be used wisely, not to be used for frightening large animals on the ark. But what Samson didn't know was that he wasn't the most feared creature on the ark. . . .

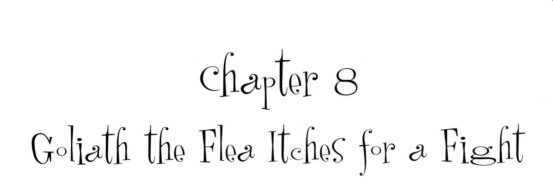

Chapter 8
Goliath the Flea Itches for a Fight

For such a tiny creature, Goliath the Flea was quickly becoming a big, big problem.

Abraham the Polar Bear had an itch—in the middle of his back, right between his shoulders—that was driving him crazy. First, he backed up against a rough pole and scratched against it up and down and from side to side and grumbled low and long: "Rowwwwowwwowww!" But when he stopped, the itch was still there. "Arrrggghh!" So he rolled onto the ground, paws straight up, and wiggled and wriggled across the floor of the ark, kicking up a cloud of straw dust.

Nearby, a wolf and a coyote saw what was happening. "What's up with him?" asked the coyote.

The wolf shook his head pitifully—he'd seen this kind of behavior before. "Ah, it's Goliath."

"Goliath?"

"Yes," the wolf said. "Goliath the Flea. He's terrorizing all of us. Gave me fits for three days. Couldn't sleep. Just moaned and scratched all day."

"How'd you get rid of him?"

The wolf looked at the coyote as if he'd gone crazy. "You don't get rid of Goliath. He comes and goes as he pleases, pesters whomever he pleases, and stays as long as he wants." Then the wolf shook his head and laughed. "Get rid of Goliath indeed. Ha!"

Then the voice of Abraham the Polar Bear called out, "Whoever can rid me of Goliath, I will fetch him straw for his bed; I

will bring him food to eat; I will give him polar bear rides for free!" And he might have gone on and on with enough promises fit for a king, but he had found a gate latch, had backed up to it, and was trying to press the sharp part of the latch into his thick fur to attack the flea. But not even this would work.

The offer was pretty tempting, so the wolf looked at the coyote and asked, "Want to give it a try?"

But the coyote shook his head. "Goliath's too small. I'd wear down my claws trying to track down the little beggar."

"Yeah, that's what I was thinking."

Then the wolf and coyote thought for a while about how to help the tortured polar bear. It wasn't long, though, before they were thinking with their eyes closed, and soon they were asleep.

Soon they were awakened by a little shepherd dog named David. "Hey, everybody," he called to his brothers, "I brought you something to eat." The wolf and the coyote gobbled down the food while the shepherd dog watched in amazement as the polar bear used a pitch fork as a back scratcher. "What's wrong with him?"

"Goliath the Flea," answered the wolf with his mouth full.

"Too bad we can't help," said coyote. "I could use more straw under my bed."

"But it's just a flea," said David. "We scratch away fleas all the time. And just look at poor Abraham." The polar bear had stacked up several bales of hay now and had propped the pitchfork between the top two bales so that the sharp points stuck out at just the right height.

"Not *this* flea, you don't," said the wolf, with a touch of fear in his voice. "He's too small, not just small—tiny!"

"Teeny-tiny," agreed the coyote.

"We'd wear ourselves out try-ing to find him," added the wolf. "And then the next thing you

know we'll be rolling around on the floor and looking silly like Abraham."

"I'll do it," said David. "I'll get rid of Goliath."

The wolf looked at the coyote. Then he turned to David and said, "You're too big, brother. Why, Goliath will pounce on you and not let up for days. You'll go mad!"

But David wouldn't listen to his brothers. He approached the polar bear slowly. "Are you here to help?" Abraham asked. Now the bear was trying to stretch his arms around to his back and reach the itchy spot, but no matter how much he tried, there was always one spot his claws wouldn't reach. "If so," continued Abraham, "the pitchfork is right over there." He pointed. "Just grab hold of the handle and do the best you can. I could sure use some relief."

But the pitchfork was too heavy for David, so he dropped it. Then he turned to Abraham and said, "Look, God gave me a set of these," and with that said, David held forth his paw and his shiny, long claws glistened in the lamplight. Abraham's eyes widened. He seemed pleased.

"Show me where," David said.

So Abraham reached the furthest he'd ever reached and pointed right to a small spot between his shoulders. With a sudden flurry, David the Shepherd Dog scratched the old bear's back better than any pitchfork, post, or bale of straw could ever do. When he was finished, Abraham stood straight, paused, and then smiled. With a great big nod, and without any more scratching, he exclaimed, "You did it! You knocked off Goliath!"

David the Shepherd Dog wagged his head and thanked God, the one who had made his claws, including the tiny little points that could scratch away an even tinier little critter.

Somewhere in the ark, in a crack in the floor, on a speck of dust, paced a tiny flea named Goliath. "I don't understand," said the flea, as he paced back and forth. "How could that simple dog find me so quickly? I'm trained at this sort of thing. All he does is chase sheep!"

"Now, now, Goliath," said Mrs. Flea. "So you had a bad day. But let's not lose our head over this one little instance."

The tiny little flea plopped down, slapped his forehead with all six hands, and groaned a giant groan.

That was the worst day in the little flea's short life—that is until the day he almost drowned because of a certain giraffe. . . .

Chapter 9
Daniel the Giraffe Opens a Window

Darius the Lion, known by all as King of the Jungle before all this flooding business, looked up, up, up the long, golden neck of the giraffe and, with water pouring into his face, shouted at the top of his lungs, "DANIEL! CLOSE THAT WINDOW AND GET INSIDE BEFORE YOU DROWN US ALL!"

Daniel did this all the time—opened the little window, which was up so high that only he could reach it, and poked his head outside. "I just can't stand to be cooped up day-in and day-out," explained the giraffe. "If I don't stretch from time to time, I'll wind up with the worst crick in my neck. Ever have one of those really bad cricks that just makes you want to scream?" He rubbed his neck against a tall pole.

"I know, Daniel," said the lion, "but we're all down here getting soaked. And none of us likes to get soaked—except maybe for the hippos, but never mind them.

"Just give me a minute," called the giraffe. And from where Darius the Lion stood, he could barely make out the giraffe's face as rainwater covered him like a sheet, and much of it ran down his long neck to puddle on the floor next to Darius.

When Darius the Lion went back to his straw, all wet and smelly now, many of those around him demanded that he do something.

"For crying out loud," said the aardvark, "I've got a nose longer than anyone else here, but you don't see me complaining about being too cramped. Too wet? Yes. So why don't you make him close the window?"

"Yeah," joined in the porcupine. "Every drop is like a sharp needle on my back."

And so the complaints went on and on, until one day Darius had no choice but to try to force Daniel to come in out of the rain.

He stood next to his towering friend and called, "Okay, Daniel, show's over. Time to come in and close up the window." But the giraffe didn't budge. "Daniel, my friend, it's time to come in and—"

"Have you ever tried this?" called down the giraffe.

"You mean sticking my head out in the rain?" asked Darius. "No."

The giraffe just laughed into the wind, stretching his neck out even further. "You've got to try this, Darius. Sure it's a little wet. Sure it's a little windy. But you're right up here next to God. Come on."

That was a good speech, thought the lion. So why not give it a try? "But how?" he asked, looking up so high.

The giraffe shook his neck muscles and said, "Climb on."

And so the lion, without using his claws of course, hopped up on the giraffe's back and then, with all the skill of a lion in the jungle, skill that showed why he was called King of the Jungle, climbed right up the backbone of the giraffe, until he was at the opening that led to the roof. He took a deep breath, as if he were diving into a lake rather than simply poking his head into the rain, and soon found himself cheek-to-cheek with Daniel.

The rain soaked him. The wind howled in his ears. But Daniel was right: Up here high, with the elements swirling about his head, Darius felt closer to God than he had ever felt. He hung on to the giraffe's neck even tighter, and together they laughed and laughed and swallowed lots of rainwater.

Eventually Darius had to slide back down his friend's neck and go back into the ark. He went back to his friends, who were still sort of wet and not very pleased at how things had gone, or at how Darius was handling this situation.

"Well?" said the porcupine. "Any luck with Daniel?"

"Yeah," added the aardvark. "If I catch a head cold, it's big trouble for all of us."

"I've got a great idea," the lion said. And with that, he walked over to Daniel, beckoned for the giraffe to lean down, and whispered to his friend.

"Okay," called Darius, "who wants to be first?"

The porcupine shyly walked up to Daniel, as the giraffe low-ered his head to the ground. The porcupine climbed up, and Daniel straightened his head, lifting the smaller animal right up to the window. As rain drenched the porcupine, he giggled with delight. "This is great!" he shouted to the others below him.

That was all it took. The animals couldn't get to Daniel fast enough. The smaller

ones rode on his head, while the larger ones climbed up the giraffe's neck, as Darius had done.

Daniel had started something that might have gone on for quite a long time if not for the most shocking event of all: the rain suddenly stopped! And for the first time in days and days and days the sun came out, shining brilliantly from behind the clouds. Everyone was silent. Not a *bray*, not a *whinny*, nor *growl* nor *cluck* nor *tweet* came from anywhere on the ark. For a moment there was complete and total silence, until it was shattered by the loudest shout any of them had ever heard before. And everyone who heard knew that the noise had come from the very throat of Noah himself.

It was Daniel who spoke first: "Whatever you do, my friends," he said, pulling his head in for the first time in a long time, "never forget the feel of the rain on your face. Sometimes its cold and can sting or make you sneeze, but when you feel closer to God, isn't it worth it all?"

After a long, thoughtful moment of silence, Darius roared a kingly roar and everyone else joined in to say thank you to Daniel.

Before long, Noah and his sons had opened all the other windows that were still latched. A fresh wind blew through, and, best of all, beams of sunlight, like long golden fingers, poked through from the ceiling and the sides of the ark to reach the once dark spaces. And as the ark floated on, now only much calmer, Daniel the Giraffe lay with his head resting on a pile of soft straw. And where he lay, a golden shaft of sunlight shone down and warmed the top of his head. Next to him was Darius the Lion, sleeping soundly with one big paw resting on his friend's long, golden neck.

The animals were so happy to finally see the sun. They were already dreaming about their new homes. So why was everyone afraid to leave the ark when it landed? And what in the world was that scary noise? . . .

Chapter 10
The Dark, Scary Secret of the Doves

W hat was that noise?" asked Mrs. Turtle.

Mr. Turtle had just fallen asleep when his wife shook him awake. He listened for a moment and said, "Which noise? Do you mean the high-pitched, whistling, whirring sound or the low-pitched, grumbling growl? Or maybe you're talking about the gurgling, bubbling, whooshing sound."

Mrs. Turtle rolled her eyes. "Not those sounds. I've heard all those plenty. This is a new noise. So different, so—" Mrs. Turtle shivered. "—so scary."

Mr. Turtle poked out his head and legs from his shell and said, "Okay, I'll go check it out, but I'm telling you, it's probably that camel again or—"

SCREE! SCREE! SCREEEEEEEE!

"What in the ark was that!?" said Mr. Turtle.

"That's what I was talking about," whispered Mrs. Turtle. And rather than get out of his soft bed and check things out, Mr. Turtle settled back deeper and deeper into his shell, until all anyone could see of him was his little beady eyes.

The next morning the ark was abuzz with talk about the new noise.

"Am I the only one who got goose bumps?" asked Jael the Goose.

"Hey, maybe I didn't get goose bumps," said Gideon the Beaver, "but I nearly broke off a tooth the first time I heard it."

"We need to find Noah," said Jehoshaphat the Yak. "He'll take care of it."

"I tell you what," spoke up Samson the Skunk. "If you just tell me where it came from, I'll take care of everything." And with that he waved his long, striped tail back and forth.

Daniel the Giraffe said something, but no one could really tell what, because he had poked his head through the high small window.

"It seems as though I've heard something like this before," said Esther the Ostrich, and she stared off at the ceiling, thinking hard about where that might have been.

"Hey, everybody!" shouted Moses the Ferret, chittering excitedly like ferrets do when they get too excited. "The

door's open! The door's open! Noah's opened the door! It's time to go out!"

And there might have been a stampede for the door had not—in that second of silence between the last word the ferret shouted and the instant they could have bolted—someone said, "Suppose the noise came from *outside?*"

So instead of racing out into the sunshine and the sweet, green grass, everyone huddled closer together, and even the polar bears admitted that they had goose bumps.

Samson the Skunk was just telling everyone again how, if he only knew where the noise was coming from, he'd take care of the problem, when suddenly his little speech was cut short by the now familiar noise: *SCREE! SCREE! SCREEEEE!*

Everyone hushed. The silence was thick as the black goo on the side of the ark, and the only thing that broke it was the sound of footfalls coming down the ramp and, of course, *SCREE! SCREE! SCREEEEE!* Grunts, snorts, and cackles were stuck in the throats of those all huddled together. The area by the ramp was dark and shadowy. But soon all were able to see an even darker shadow moving, flowing down the ramp, coming closer to them. *SCREE! SCREE! SCREEEEE!*

Slowly the shadow began to take form and . . . and . . . and there seemed to be a collective sighing grunt as Noah himself emerged from the shadows, up close and smiling. In his hands he held something small. And on either shoulder sat a gray turtle dove.

"Well, well, my friends," came the pleasant, soothing voice of Noah. "Why are you still here and not racing out into the brand-new world?"

SCREE! SCREE! SCREEEEEE! came the giant sound from the something small in Noah's cupped hands, and all eyes seemed to be focused there. "Don't be afraid, my friends," said Noah. "God has brought us to the end of our journey and has protected us completely. He's held us for these many, many days, just as I am holding this." And now Noah opened his hands to reveal a tiny, featherless bird with a big beak and gaping mouth. *SCREE! SCREE! SCREEEEEE!* "Why, this new little creature belongs to the turtle doves here," he said, smiling so big that the room seemed to light up. "Now come

on.

Let's go

outside." Then he

turned and, with the turtle

doves on his shoulders,

walked to the edge of the

sunny opening. He spoke

to the birds on his shoul-

ders: "Adam and Eve, why

don't you show us the way off

this boat." And the birds

flew from his shoul-

ders and out the

door, and, for a

few moments, at least until the rest of the gang could lumber down the ramp, Adam and Eve were the only two living things in the new world. "Hey," called Noah, holding out the baby bird still too young to fly, "don't forget this one!"

"I thought I'd heard that sound before," said Esther the Ostrich, as she made her way down the ramp with the others. "Cousin Turtle Dove."

Samson swung his striped tail as he waddled off and said, "For such a little thing he sure did raise a lot of *cain*."

"Yes," agreed Mrs. Porcupine. "You wouldn't think such a little thing would be *able* to make that much noise."

And as the animals moved out in all different directions, just as they had come in, one small voice could be heard weaving its way in and out among hooves and paws, that of a ferret: "Zipporah? Zipporah? Now where'd you go off to? You can't go wandering off like this. This place is just too big for that. . . ."

I have put my rainbow
in the clouds and it will be the
sign of the covenant between
me and the earth.

Genesis 9:13

(NIrV)